Sammy Squirrel & Rodney Raccoon

To The Rescue

Sammy Squirrel & Rodney Raccoon
To The Rescue

by Duane Lawrence
illustrations by Gordon Clover

Book layout and cover design: Jamie Fischer
from series design by Momentum Productions

Printed in Canada

Library and Archives Canada Cataloguing in Publication

Lawrence, Duane, 1956-
      Sammy Squirrel & Rodney Raccoon
to the rescue / Duane Lawrence.

ISBN 978-1-894694-98-8

  I. Title. II. Title: Sammy Squirrel and Rodney
Raccoon to the rescue.

PS8573.A904S233 2011   jC813'.6   C2011-902253-2

Granville Island Publishing
212 – 1656 Duranleau
Vancouver, BC, Canada V6H 3S4
Tel: (604) 688-0320 Toll free: 1-877-688-0320
www.GranvilleIslandPublishing.com

To Bert and Grace

Contents

1

Visions of Nuts
and Marshmallows

It was a brilliant morning in Stanley Park, and most of the animal residents were out and about enjoying the sun. The beavers at Beaver Lake were rebuilding and renovating while the good weather lasted. The ducks, geese, swans and other waterfowl at Lost Lagoon were busy gliding and parading. Frogs were leaping in the ponds, rabbits were hopping in the woods, birds were singing in the treetops, and Sammy Squirrel was on his way back to his tree house deep in the heart of the park.

Sammy had spent the early part of the morning nut hunting near Prospect Point. Then he had buried his nut treasures in several well-chosen spots throughout the woods and noted each location carefully to ensure that he would remember it later so as to avoid the very embarrassing predicament of a squirrel being unable to find his nut haul. That job completed, Sammy had joined a few park friends in a game of Nutter, which is something like soccer, but a big round nut is used instead of a ball. Herman Heron acted as the referee while Gordon Goose, Tony Turtle, Benjamin Beaver, Simone Swan and even Dolores Duck had joined in the fun.

Sammy liked to be busy and productive, but found that if his morning was full of activity he needed to balance it with a quieter afternoon. Upon returning home, he made himself a pot of green leaf tea and settled into his armchair with a book. His favourite author, Magpie Indawood, had just published a new novel whose plot gripped the reader with a marvellous dramatic intensity. Sammy found it impossible to stop reading and stayed in his chair the whole afternoon, book in one hand... teacup in the other.

But the sunlight, which had filtered its way around the trees and through his tree house windows, had now begun to fade.

It's hard to read in the dim light of late afternoon, Sammy thought and frowned, since he really didn't want to put this book down. *Crow's Beak* was a captivating story about a famous old crow who was kidnapped... or crow-napped, to be more precise.

Well, I'll just have to finish it later, he thought, reluctantly

putting the book down and moving toward the window where the view from the upper reaches of his tall Douglas fir tree was spectacular. The sunlight still glittered and glowed between the ancient cedars, massive firs and gorgeous maple trees. Then a gentle wind began to sway the large tree branches lightly so that they appeared to be waving at him.

"Hello trees, hello woods, hello greenery!" Sammy exclaimed. And although he knew the trees couldn't answer back, he often had a feeling at moments like this that they had somehow heard him.

Suddenly, Sammy remembered that he had promised to meet his friend Rodney Raccoon at the new animal café in the park that afternoon. It had completely slipped his mind and now he was late.

Poor Rodney will be waiting and maybe even worrying that some terrible thing has happened to me.

So without a moment's delay, for Sammy was quick to act once he made a decision, he scampered out the door, down the tree and along the narrow animal path to meet his dear friend.

Although Sammy's day had started productively, Rodney had spent the morning curled up in his lair reading his favourite book, *The Omnivore's Guide to Eating Everything.* Rodney wasn't exactly sure what the word 'omnivore' meant, but he was convinced that he was one because he loved to eat just about anything he could get his paws on. And having spent most of the morning reading about food, Rodney had worked up quite an appetite.

My goodness, it's almost noon, he thought. *I should really start thinking about lunch!*

Lunch was a difficult time for Rodney because it required making a decision from several options — all of them delectable. There were berries of infinite variety along the trails, probably marshmallows left under the bridge at Lost Lagoon and clams to be dug and eaten along the shores of the enormous park.

"Decisions, decisions, decisions," muttered Rodney. "My life seems to be governed by difficult decisions." But his stomach was now in command; so Rodney put down the book and left his lair without really knowing where his appetite would lead him.

The air was fresh, the sky was a radiant blue, and everything outside Rodney's lair was gorgeously green.

Could there be a better park for any civilized animal to be in at this very moment? he wondered.

Rodney often asked himself questions like that and sometimes felt he should have been a philosopher, dispensing wisdom to all the moaners and groaners of this vast park who never seemed able to appreciate the beauty all around them. And as he meandered down the well-trodden trail away from his lair, he imagined himself pouring out buckets of words of wisdom at Old Hollow Hall, the ancient hollow tree the park animals used as their community centre.

"Stop your moaning and groaning and listen to me," Rodney orated, all the while picturing the other animals listening in awe as he read from his book of wisdom. Lost in this magnificent fantasy, Rodney continued exclaiming without noticing the very real bird that now stood directly in front of him.

"Just what do you mean by that?" squawked Penelope Pigeon, bringing Rodney back to his senses with a lurch.

"What do I mean by what?" Rodney asked.

"By what you just said!" Penelope replied.

"And what was it I said?"

"That if I stopped all my moaning and groaning and listened to you, I would find the secret to happiness."

"Oh, did I say that? Well, I wasn't saying it to you personally, Penelope. I was…I was…saying it to all the animals gathered at Old Hollow Hall who were there to hear me…read from my new book on…uh…enlighten-ment, I suppose," Rodney explained rather awkwardly and incompletely.

"Oh, were you now…because I could have sworn you

were on the animal trail leading to Lost Lagoon talking about nothing. How could I have been so mistaken?"

"Well, perhaps, um —"

"Old Hollow Hall indeed!" Penelope sputtered with anger. "Rodney Raccoon, you have been eating too many of those marshmallows left under the bridge, and they've turned your brain soft."

"Well, I didn't really think I was *actually* at Old Hollow Hall. I mean, I was just…well…thinking that if I *were* there…of course I'm not, I know…but *if* I were…and had written a book, then —"

"Enough!" Penelope said sharply. "Wherever you think you are…or were…I hope you have a good time there because, like most of the other animals in this park, I have to go to work! Whereas all you do is wait under bridges for marshmallow hand-outs or rob the bushes of their beautiful berries. Humph!" Then she flapped her wings and flew over the bushes to her next tap-dancing gig along the seawall, where she hoped to earn a bit of food from the people who appreciated real art.

"Penelope is so rude!" mumbled Rodney as he continued down the trail. "Very uncivilized…and such a pouty pigeon too. Pigeons aren't really park animals anyway, since they just hang around the outskirts of the park," he grumbled as he moseyed along. "I really *should* write a book about proper manners and address it to pigeons in particular."

Now, where was I going? Rodney suddenly thought. *Oh my goodness and gosh. I'm supposed to meet Sammy at the Argyle Café!* So Rodney turned off the animal trail and entered the path to Beaver Lake. And as he passed the arched bridge at Lost Lagoon, the smell of marshmallows replaced his visions of glory and fame.

2

Surprised at the Argyle Café

The Argyle Café was very new. It had just opened in the trunk of an old fir tree near Beaver Lake. Everything about the Argyle was unusual — its name, its owner and its décor. The new proprietor, Reginald Rat, was originally from some faraway place called Scotland. He had stowed away on a large ship to come to Canada and now made his home in Stanley Park.

Reggie had a fascination for argyle things, meaning that he liked anything woven with diamond-shaped patterns on it. Hence, he and the café workers all wore argyle vests, the curtains and table mats were argyle and there were framed posters of argyle patterns in a surprising array of different colours on the café wall.

This was the first time for Sammy at the Argyle. Rodney had been a few times now and had found the clam chowder quite enchanting. In fact, he was in the middle of a bowl of chowder when Sammy rushed in and sat down.

"Terribly sorry, Rodney. Just got carried away with a good book and forgot about the real world for awhile," said Sammy.

"Not to worry, friend," said Rodney. "I was off in another world a bit myself earlier today. But never mind about that. What's the name of that novel you're reading? *Fish's Fin,* or *Duck's Waddle* or *Goat's Grin*…something like that, isn't it?"

"The name of the book is *Crow's Beak.* You picked it up and looked at it the other day at my house, remember?" Sammy said, slightly annoyed. "You should read it. It's really quite thrilling!"

"My life is quite thrilling enough, thank you very much," replied Rodney.

Sammy ordered hazelnut coffee, and Rodney ordered another bowl of clam chowder. Not that he was so terribly hungry, but it would clearly have been impolite to sit there with nothing while his friend drank a cup of coffee.

"I couldn't help but overhear you two discussing books. Are you writers?" inquired Reggie Rat after he took their orders.

"No, we're readers, actually," replied Sammy. "Have you ever heard of Magpie Indawood? I've got her latest

18

novel and I must say it's excellent."

"Magpie Indawood…yes, she is a marvellous writer," said Reggie. "Her latest book is about a crow-napping. Such a coincidence, isn't it?"

"What coincidence?" asked Sammy.

"Why, Judy Crow has just been crow-napped from Stanley Park. All the local crows are in a panic, thinking they might be next. The whole park is talking about it. A few ducks at Lost Lagoon said they saw two large crows flying out of the park toward the city pulling Judy behind them."

"Crow-napped…oh my goodness!" said Rodney.

"Some park herons say they saw the three of them land near the Sylvia Hotel at English Bay."

"That hotel is for people, isn't it? Why would they go near a place like that?"

"Well, there's the Animal Inn under the Sylvia Hotel. Maybe they've taken her there. The entrance to the inn is hidden at the back of the hotel."

"Judy is the crabbiest crow I know. Why would any sane bird want to crow-nap her?" wondered Rodney. "She's always insisting that we all call her Judith Raven, since it sounds more posh than Judy Crow. Well, I say, good riddance to her!"

"That's enough, Rodney," said Sammy. "Judy is our friend and always has been. No one's perfect. Look at yourself: you eat too much and you're lazy. That's what the other animals say, but they still treat you as a friend."

"Eating is important! You can't eat too much. And how can they call me lazy when I'm always busy looking for food?" asked Rodney with a hurt look.

"Because you never do any work…but never mind that. One of our park companions has been crow-napped!" Sammy gasped. "Can you believe that? I wish we could help somehow. I really do."

Sammy and Rodney said good-bye to Reggie and complimented him on the argyle décor while they paid their bill. Both little animals were deep in thought as they left the café.

"So, I suppose you want to go into the city now, don't you? You want to be some kind of hero and find Judy Crow, right?" Rodney asked.

"She's our friend, Rodney. Surely we can do something."

"Don't try to be a big hero, Sammy. What good can come out of that? It'll just get us into trouble."

"Rodney, you sound like most of the animals around here. 'Let someone else take care of things…what can a little animal like me do…why should I try?' Isn't that what they all say? Well, maybe that kind of thinking is wrong. Isn't it important for an animal to stand up for a friend and do the right thing?"

"I don't know, Sammy. So many things could go wrong."

They walked on in silence, both recalling the time they had wanted to go to Vancouver to discover what the world of people and pets was really like. But they had ended up lost at sea instead…and wound up in *Japan,* where they helped resolve a crisis for some Japanese deer. They had been lucky to return safely home.

"If we could help those Japanese deer," Sammy said, "surely we can help a Canadian crow." The two friends stopped walking and looked at each other. Rodney looked away for a moment, then looked back at Sammy.

"All right!" he blurted out.

"I knew you'd want to do the right thing. You're a good raccoon, my friend!" said Sammy.

"I just hope we don't get knocked off course and end up in a foreign country again."

"We won't. We'll help someone in our own country," said Sammy. "We'll find her. I know we can."

3

On Their Way

The next morning at sunrise Sammy and Rodney set out for Vancouver. Although there were several ancient animal trails that wound their way toward the city, the two friends chose to take the one they had started on many years ago in their first attempt to visit Vancouver.

It was a sunny and tranquil summer morning in Stanley Park. The two animals tramped along, breathing in the fresh park air that was now and again scented with moss or with ferns and grass or with cedar, depending on how hard and in which direction the wind blew. Even though Sammy and Rodney had lived here all of their lives, the majestic fir and cedar trees that towered over them still evoked a sense of deep respect and awe. The two little friends were constantly humbled by the presence of these mysterious and ancient giants that shaded, housed and protected them and all the other park animals. Grateful to be residents of such a magnificent place, Sammy and Rodney continued their trek in rapturous silence.

Out of the blue, Renee Rabbit appeared on the trail and squinted at Sammy and Rodney. Reaching into her bag, she took out her glasses and put them on to get a better look.

"Well, if it isn't Sammy Squirrel and Rodney Raccoon," she said warmly. "I thought you two were tree stumps for a moment; but you were moving, so I knew you couldn't be. Stumps tend to stay put, as we all know, unless they're dragged away by humans."

"Hello, Renee," said Sammy. "You know, you really should wear your glasses all the time. You might have an accident one day."

"Oh, I suppose you're right," she replied. "But my glasses fall off when I'm hopping, and you both know I do a lot of hopping around this huge park of ours. The only time I can keep my glasses on my nose is when I stop. Where are you two going so early in the morning?"

"Judy Crow has been crow-napped. We're going to try to find her," said Rodney.

"My goodness…crow-napped!" exclaimed Renee. "But you're not detectives of any kind. What makes you think you can help?"

"We'll just do our best. What else can one do?" asked Sammy.

"One can only do one's best, can't one?" remarked Renee. "And two can do double the work of one! But hopping around a city trying to find crow-nappers with all those people and pets everywhere…it's quite frightening. I really don't think you should be doing this."

"But we can't just let her be crow-napped," said Sammy.

"I'm not saying you should…but what if something equally terrible happens to you? Years ago, my father told me about a series of tunnels that go from Stanley Park into the city. Some rabbit friends of his went exploring through them and never returned!"

"But we're not taking any tunnels, Renee," explained Rodney.

"Precisely my point…because it's even more dangerous to go there above ground. Why, I've even heard stories of unleashed dogs roaming the city streets looking for unsuspecting animals like us."

"I suppose it's risky, Renee. But we have to go. It's the right thing to do," said Sammy.

"If you must do this, please…be careful, won't you?"

"We promise, Renee," said Sammy. "Well, we mustn't delay. Now, do watch where you're hopping."

Renee put her
glasses back in her bag
and turned toward the woods. The
vegetation was so thick she disappeared
from view as soon as she left the animal path.

As Sammy and Rodney continued their
journey, they saw a radiant blue colour in the
distance between the trees. It was the Great
Ocean, and it never ceased to excite them when-
ever they caught glimpses of it along this particular
trail. The Great Ocean sparkled and shimmered,
disappearing now and again behind the trees as if
it were playing hide-and-seek with the two little animals.

A while later they arrived at a cliff edge and looked
out at the Great Ocean in all its vastness, glittering and
glimmering like a thousand jewels. They drank in the

view and gazed down at the seawall path, which
hadn't filled with people and pets yet. But soon it would
be, as rush hour — or so the animals liked to call it —
came to Stanley Park and the seawall became a
frenzied mass of people —
often attached by leashes
to their pets — rushing
around on foot, on
skates and on bicycles.

Sammy and Rodney made their way down the zigzag trail toward the seawall. When they reached the bottom, they stopped behind a large wall of huckleberry bushes that marked the boundary between the seawall path and the woods. Before heading along the hidden animal trail that led into the city, they looked through a natural arbour in the bushes that opened onto the seawall. They could see the sandy beach and the sparkling ocean, framed like a picture by the arched opening. Both of the little animals sighed as they remembered their first adventure, that began on this very beach many years ago.

They turned away from the view and ambled along the hidden animal trail toward the city. The trail went this way and that, up hills and down, sometimes beside the seawall, sometimes veering away from it and back into the park. After a great deal of meandering in this fashion, they came upon Squirty Skunk sitting on a stump at the side of the trail.

"Good morning, Squirty," said Rodney, while Sammy smiled and nodded his head in greeting.

"Good morning, fellow park animals," he replied. "Where in the world would you two be going on such a beautiful day?"

"We're off to Vancouver," said Rodney. "We're going to find Judy Crow. She's been crow-napped, you know."

"Yes, I've heard about it. Terrible thing. How do you propose to find her?"

"She was seen being hauled across the sky over the park," Sammy said. "Apparently they landed near the Animal Inn at English Bay. We're told it's not too far from the edge of the park."

"Be very careful, my friends. This could be a dangerous undertaking. Crow-nappers are unlikely to be kind, and you're not familiar with Vancouver. Should you need to fend off the villains, I can squirt them with my skunky scent. In fact, the more I think about it, the more I feel I should go with you. I'd have to check with Mrs. Skunk first, of course."

"Thanks for your offer, Squirty, but we just don't have the time to wait. The longer we delay, the harder it will be to find Judy Crow."

"I wish you'd told me earlier that you were going. Best of luck, you two!"

"Thank you, Squirty," said Rodney. "Um, you wouldn't happen to have a bit of food you could share, would you?"

"Stop it, Rodney," said Sammy. "We must be on our way, Squirty. Good-bye!"

Although Sammy and Rodney knew you couldn't generalize about any animal group, most of the skunks they encountered in the park were somewhat aloof. Squirty, however, was always very kind and sociable.

The two friends walked on for hours, until what had begun as an early morning jaunt became a late afternoon trek. The walk to Vancouver was taking longer than they had imagined, and both began wondering if they would ever arrive.

A little while later they turned a corner along the trail and found themselves at the edge of Stanley Park. Sammy and Rodney saw the city of Vancouver for the first time. English Bay beach was to their right, marking the very edge of the Great Ocean. To their left they saw gigantic buildings which made them gasp. The buildings were much taller than the cedar and fir trees in the park but lacked the great dignity and majesty of the trees. Directly ahead, there appeared to be a small green, squarish mountain with a rather flat top. It seemed to be a natural landmark in the area, so Sammy and Rodney decided to go over and climb it to get a better view of things.

As they approached the mountain with the flat top, they noticed a peculiar thing. The little mountain appeared to have windows all over it.

"Isn't that the strangest thing," said Rodney. "I could have sworn from back there that was a weird little mountain. But it's a building with green vines all over it.

Quite attractive, really. Don't you think so?"

"I do indeed," agreed Sammy. "Nothing like a bit of greenery…or even a lot of it…to make a place look attractive. You know, the name of that type of vine is Virginia creeper. I've read about it in *A Squirrel's Guide to Greenery*. Don't see much of that kind of vine in the park, do we?" Then he noticed the sign at the front of the building.

"Well, what do you know," he said, pleasantly surprised. "Look at the sign, Rodney. It's the Sylvia Hotel…exactly the place we're looking for. Now that is serendipity."

"That's what? That's syrupy? You mean, it's like syrup?" asked Rodney. Suddenly he felt a pang of hunger. "Do you feel like having pancakes with syrup, Sammy? I'm a bit peckish after all this walking."

"I didn't say 'syrupy.' I said 'serendipity.' It means to make a fortunate discovery by chance," replied Sammy.

"Oh, yes…of course that's what it means. I knew that," said Rodney. "Just forgot for a moment. Now, how about those pancakes and syrup? After we check in at the Animal Inn, we can have something to eat." Rodney made a mental note that he should look up the word 'serendipity' as soon as he got home.

4

A Midnight Mystery

Sammy and Rodney walked to the back of the Sylvia Hotel, where they found the little arched door hidden by shrubs and bushes. They entered the Animal Inn and were greeted by a small fox whose name tag read "Fernando."

"Welcome to the Animal Inn, friends," said Fernando Fox with a kind smile. "And what name is your reservation under?"

"Reservation? We don't have one," replied Sammy.

"Well, that is a problem, I'm afraid. There's a convention of marmots from Vancouver Island here and we're completely booked."

"But we have nowhere else to go," said Rodney, "and we're hungry."

"And we're on an urgent mission to save Judy Crow.

She's been crow-napped, you know," Sammy added.

"Well, goodness me, I'm so sorry, but…wait, we do have a couple of tiny rooms at the very end of the hall that the marmots weren't interested in. To be honest, marmots are a bit cheap and like to pack six to a room. No way six of them could fit into these rooms, so they didn't want them. They're not fancy, and as I've said, they're very small. Are you interested?"

"We'll share a small room to economize," said Sammy.

After checking in, Sammy and Rodney walked down to their room to have a look. Then they headed for the inn's restaurant to enjoy some pancakes and syrup. Food had been on Rodney's mind ever since Sammy had mentioned that long syrupy-sounding word when they were in front of the hotel. Rodney thoroughly enjoyed the delicious pancakes and reminded himself again to look up that long 's' word when he got back to his lair — if only he could remember what that word was!

Sammy tried to make polite dinner conversation, as any civilized animal would, but his gaze wandered. He kept hoping to see Judy Crow and hear her cawing loudly and demanding that everyone in the place call her Judith Raven. His eyes roamed the room, but there wasn't a single crow in sight.

After dinner the two little friends were quite weary. It

had been a long journey from the deep forests of Stanley Park to the Animal Inn. They returned to their room and wished each other a good night. Rodney Raccoon opened a window to let in the fresh air. Then he flopped onto the bed, and before he could say to himself the 'Gosh' part of 'Gosh, I'm tired,' he fell soundly asleep.

During the night it started to rain and the wind began to blow. It wasn't a heavy storm, but the pitter-patter of the rain and the whoosh-whoosh of the wind were loud enough to draw Rodney from his slumber. As he got up to close the window, he heard an unusual sound. At first he thought it was the wind, but he gradually realized that it was coming from inside the inn.

Rodney put his ear to the wall of the room and listened intently. A faint voice called out for help...then suddenly stopped.

Was that Judy? Rodney wondered, and decided he should wake up Sammy immediately. Then the two of them could track down the desperate voice.

"Did you hear it, Sammy?" he queried as he gave him a shake. "Did you hear a mysterious voice calling for help?"

"I did. Faintly, though," replied Sammy, opening his eyes. "I was half-asleep, but thought I'd heard something odd. Do you think it's Judy Crow?"

"I do, and she's probably somewhere in the inn. Let's

go and have a look around."

Sammy and Rodney entered the corridor and tiptoed past several doors until they came to the end of the hall. Turning the corner, they were surprised to find three long tunnels in front of them that veered off at different angles, winding this way and that into the distance.

"How strange," Rodney said. "What are tunnels doing here? What kind of inn is this anyway?"

"This must be the series of tunnels that Renee Rabbit was talking about. The owners of the Animal Inn probably dug out rooms along these tunnels to make the inn bigger."

"Those little business beasts are smart, aren't they? But it gets a bit confusing down here. Our friend Renee would be going in circles in this place, even with her glasses on!"

"I doubt that many guests stay in the rooms this far down. Anyway, why don't you go down the path to the left for a bit and see what you can find. I'll take the path to the right, and we'll meet back here then explore the middle route together."

"Maybe we should go back and have a snack first."

"What? You're hungry — in the middle of the night?"

"Well, we're about to wander down long, nearly dark corridors that appear to be endless. So…wouldn't it be a good plan to get a bit of food first?"

"No, Rodney, it would not! We'll eat later. Now off you go to the left. We'll meet back here in five minutes."

Rodney gave his friend an angry look, then turned and walked slowly down the left tunnel. "Only a nut…that eats mainly nuts…wouldn't want to have a good meal first," he mumbled to himself.

As Rodney grumbled his way along the path, it became darker and harder to see the farther he went. *Mustn't trip and fall,* he thought, slowing his pace a bit. *No, no, no, that wouldn't do at all.*

He turned this way and that along the serpentine path until he noticed a door ahead. *Either I go in and look around, or I go back and get Sammy,* he thought. *If I go in alone, there could be trouble. But if I go get Sammy, that means more time spent down here without any food.*

That last thought resolved things quickly, and Rodney tried the doorknob, which rattled a bit. Then he banged his fist several times on the door, causing it to rattle even more — but it remained stubbornly shut. Next, he decided to lunge at it. So he stepped back, then ran and banged up against the door…again…and again. On the third attempt, the door flew open and Rodney plunged in…in and down, down, down, because…there was no floor in the room!

5

Mortimer Mole

A moment later Rodney awoke, and what he saw in the dark surprised him. Tiny huckleberries, soft marshmallows and little clams danced in circles around his head in the air. He reached out with his left paw to grab one of the clams, and his paw went right through it. Then he grabbed at a marshmallow with the other paw but was left gripping only air again.

Flying huckleberries, floating marshmallows and spinning clams — what next? Rodney thought, slightly dazed. He swiped at the flying food again and again, then flopped onto his back in exhaustion. *I'll starve down here if I don't eat something soon.*

It was at that moment Rodney noticed he was stuck in the bottom of a dark pit.

"Help, Sammy, help!" he yelled. "I've fallen into a pit

and can't get out. Help!"

But Sammy had already made his way down the right tunnel and certainly could not hear Rodney. The tunnel Sammy was in twisted to and fro and became darker as he moved along. Other than that, he hadn't noticed anything unusual about it.

Might as well go back, he thought. *Can't see much of anything now.*

Then, all of a sudden, he heard a shuffling sound further on down the tunnel. So he flattened himself against the wall, held his breath and listened. As the shuffling got louder, Sammy heard someone or something panting along with the shuffling sound.

Maybe I should run back and get Rodney, he thought. *Maybe I…*"Ahhhhh!" gasped Sammy.

A rather rotund animal with beady eyes and brown fur towered over him, blocking the way. Sammy froze, expecting the worst.

"What kind of animal are you?" demanded the roundish beast in the dim light.

"I…I'm a squirrel…Sammy Squirrel."

"And what, Sammy Squirrel, are you doing in the depths of the Animal Inn? Explain yourself."

"I suppose I shouldn't be wandering around here at night," said Sammy sheepishly, "but my friend and I are looking for someone. And you are…?"

"Mortimer Mole. I'm on night security patrol. No one is supposed to be down this far. Who are you looking for?"

"A park friend, Judy Crow. Have you seen anyone down here tonight?"

"Not a soul, other than you. I've heard about this Judy Crow situation, though. Another mole told me a ransom note was dropped from the sky into Old Hollow Hall in the park. The crow-nappers are demanding five pounds of birdseed — each pound to be left at a different point in the park. One pound at Brockton Point, one at Prospect Point, one at Beaver Lake, one at the statue of Lord Stanley and…I've forgotten the other place."

"That's a lot of birdseed. It must be the two large crows that were seen flying away with her."

"Come to think of it, I thought I heard some crows cawing down here, but it didn't sound like cries for help. When you wander alone through tunnels all night, your imagination gets a bit wild. But no crow would go this far underground. It's just not natural."

"I suppose you're right. You must be very familiar with these tunnels."

"You mentioned you were with someone…"

"My friend, Rodney — we split up. He went down the left tunnel. Then we're going to meet and head down the middle one. What's down all these tunnels anyway?"

"Oh, more rooms and a few pits as well that used to be rabbit dens. The tunnels go on and on."

"Oh dear, if anyone could find a pit and fall in, it would be my friend. I'd better go back and see where he is."

"Be on your way, then. And when you find him, I suggest you return to your room. These tunnels are not safe for the likes of you. I say this for your own protection. You're just not the burrowing type…and you won't find your crow down here either, I'm sure."

"Thank you, Mortimer. Good night."

I hope Rodney didn't get lost…or fall into a pit! Sammy thought as he turned and started to walk back up to where he and Rodney had parted company earlier.

6

Crummy and Cruddy Crow

When Sammy arrived at the place where the tunnels split off, he thought he heard faint voices in the distance.

Must be the wind in these tunnels, he thought, *or I'm imagining things. Getting to be like that mole, and I've only been down here a short while.*

He chuckled to himself and started to walk down the left tunnel in search of Rodney. He moved cautiously on account of the dim light and thought he heard footsteps behind him at one point but turned around and saw nothing.

"Rodney, where are you?" Sammy called out.

"Here, I'm over here, down in a pit!" shouted Rodney. "Oh, thank goodness you found me!"

"Over where?" Sammy called back. But before Rodney could answer, Sammy suddenly heard a faint cawing coming from deep down the tunnel.

"I'm down here!" Rodney shouted.

"Quiet," Sammy said. "I hear crows coming this way."

Sammy stopped and listened. The cawing was getting louder.

Hide yourself, squirrel! Sammy thought. Opening the nearest door, he scurried in, shut it behind him and then listened intently.

Two large, rough-looking crows came hopping down the tunnel and stopped in front of the door Sammy had just closed behind him.

"This might be a good route to take if we have to get our prize out of here quickly," said Crummy.

"But I'm sure I heard something down this way," replied Cruddy.

"You're always hearing things. That's one of your problems."

"I swear I heard animal talk. Someone is down here."

"Well, that moronic mole could be patrolling around. Anyone who wanders alone here at night would be jabbering to himself. These tunnels give me the creeps. Let's go back and check on our prize."

"Wait a minute. What's the next thing we're supposed to do? You know…from the book."

"I've only read as far as where they do the crow-nap

and fly out to a hotel."

"Well, hurry up and finish reading the story. We have to know what we're supposed to do next — and quickly!"

While they hopped back down the tunnel to check on their prize, Sammy remained still until he could no longer hear any sounds in the hall. Then he opened the door and peeked out. "Rodney, did you hear that?" he said in a hushed voice.

"Of course I did. That's why I was silent. Do you think I wanted them to find me in a pit a few feet away? These crows are criminals, and that prize they mentioned is probably Judy Crow."

"Not only that — they mentioned a book, and I'm sure it's Magpie Indawood's."

"Never read it, so I wouldn't know."

"Well, it's the only crow-napping story I know of. And if that's how they got their idea, they're in big trouble. I'll explain later. But right now, we've got to get you out of that pit."

Sammy followed the sound of Rodney's voice to an open door and looked down.

"So there you are...oh my...quite far down. No way I can reach you."

"Go back and get Fernando Fox. He should be able

to figure out a
way to get me
out of
here."
"All
right,
I'll go find
some help.
Stay put until I
get back."
Rodney rolled his
eyes and shook his head. *Now, where exactly
would I go when I'm stuck in a pit?* he thought.

7

Following Hunches

S ammy scampered back in the direction of the hotel lobby as fast as he could. But, turning a corner, he suddenly smacked into a big wall of fur.

"What in the world are you doing now?" asked Mortimer Mole. "I thought I told you to go back to your room with that friend of yours!"

"You did say that, but we had a bit of a problem because my friend, Rodney, fell into…"

"…a pit," said Mortimer, clearly annoyed. "Of course he did. Didn't I warn you about that?"

"You did, and I'm awfully sorry about what's happened. But now we need your help, Mortimer."

"Well, let's see what we can do. Which tunnel is it?"

"The one on the left."

The two animals advanced down the left tunnel, turning this way and that, searching for the door of the room…

and pit…that Rodney was in.

Rodney, meanwhile, was in a terrible state. His hunger pangs were the worst they had ever been. He had been enduring the visions of berries, clams and marshmallows and was now afraid he was hearing voices.

"It's a riddle; it's a riddle…" the voice shouted over and over from a long way off.

It's a riddle? Rodney thought to himself. *Why would anyone say something like that? It's a riddle…hmm.*

Presently the shouting stopped, and Rodney heard footsteps coming from above as well as two whispering voices.

"It was just around here, I'm sure of it," said Sammy.

"Sammy, Sammy, I'm over here," Rodney called out when he recognized his dear friend's voice.

"Don't worry, I've brought help," said Sammy as Mortimer stepped forward and looked down at Rodney.

"Too far down for me to reach him."

"I have an idea," said Sammy. "If you sit down and put your legs over the edge of the pit, I'll crawl down and hang on to them. Rodney should be able to grab onto my tail and lift himself up to reach the doorway."

"Your friend is bigger than us, but we'll have to give it a try," said Mortimer.

Mortimer sat down and tightly gripped the door frame

to steady himself. He lowered his powerful legs over the pit edge and Sammy crawled down. Then Sammy held tight to Mortimer's legs and lowered his tail.

"I can't quite reach it," said Rodney, as he stood on tippy-toes and extended his paws up as high as he could.

"You'll have to jump and then grab my tail," said Sammy.

Rodney took a jump, reached out and latched onto Sammy's tail. Rodney's weight was an incredible burden, but Sammy was a strong, fit squirrel and was able to hang on tightly to Mortimer's legs. Rodney then extended a paw up to grab onto Mortimer's foot. He gripped the top edge of the pit with his other paw while gently placing a foot on Sammy's back for balance. He quickly lifted himself up and over to safety. Sammy then followed him up.

"Oh, thank you, thank you, thank you!" said Rodney. "I thought I was lost down there forever and…you wouldn't happen to have a snack on you, by any chance?"

"We don't have any food, Rodney. Never mind that. Did you hear the two crows talking again while I was gone?" asked Sammy.

"No, I didn't. But I thought I heard another voice shouting out, "It's a riddle…it's a riddle….""

"I wonder what that could mean…" pondered Sammy.

"Any ideas, Mortimer?"

"Not a clue. I did hear some peculiar noises earlier while on patrol, but they weren't coming from the left or right tunnels. The sounds were in the middle."

"That's it, that's it!" said Sammy excitedly.

"That's what?" said Rodney.

"In the middle!" said Sammy.

Mortimer and Rodney looked at each other, then back at Sammy.

"The voice didn't say 'It's a riddle.' My hunch is that the voice said 'In the middle.' It's a clue telling us to go down the middle path. You just couldn't hear it clearly from this pit. Don't you see?"

Rodney nodded his head, but his mind was elsewhere. He hadn't eaten for some time now, and little images of clams, berries and marshmallows again flew through the air in front of him.

"Let's go down the middle then," Sammy said.

"Let me lead the way," said Mortimer. "I know these tunnels better than any animal in the city, trust me."

8

The Middle Tunnel

Sammy, Rodney and Mortimer marched back down the left tunnel until they reached the main hallway of the inn again. Then they turned toward the middle tunnel and proceeded along it. The light grew dimmer as they plodded into the depths. The walls of the middle tunnel were made of dirt and rock, and the only sign that they were still at the inn were the doors they came across from time to time.

Suddenly, they heard a faint voice in the distance. "In the middle!" it called out. "Help!"

"You were right, Sammy," said Rodney, "and it does sound like Judy Crow."

"Shhhh," whispered Sammy. "Those two nasty crow-nappers might be around, and we don't want them to hear us coming."

As the three intrepid animals walked gingerly down

the hall, they suddenly heard voices.

"It's the crow-nappers," whispered Sammy.

"What are they saying?" asked Rodney.

"Hush…hush…" replied Sammy. The three animals stopped and put their ears to the tunnel wall.

"Tell that crazy crow to be quiet," said Crummy. "No one will hear her down here."

"Well, I did! Now what does it say in the book?" Cruddy asked.

"Wait a minute, I can only read so fast."

"Just go to the ending and find out when they pick up the ransom."

"Okay, okay…let's see…" Crummy flipped quickly through the pages of *Crow's Beak* and glanced at the last chapter. "Uh-oh…I…I…I think we gotta get outa here…and fast!"

"What are you talking about? We haven't got our ransom yet. Let me see that book."

Cruddy grabbed the book out of Crummy's talons, glanced at the page and slammed the book shut. "The crow-nappers get caught at the end of the story! Why didn't you read the whole thing before we started this, Crummy?"

"You were the one who wanted to grab Judy Crow as soon as I told you about the book, remember?"

"We've got to get outa here — right now!" yelled Cruddy.

Sammy quickly signalled to Rodney and Mortimer to hide behind two nearby doors in the hallway. Then he hid behind a third just as Cruddy opened a nearby door and peered up and down the hallway.

"No one around yet," Cruddy said. "Let's get outa here."

The two crows bolted into the hallway and started to scramble in the direction of the entrance to the inn.

"Now!" shouted Sammy, as he peered through the keyhole of his door.

Rodney threw open his door, and Crummy smacked into it with a thud. Mortimer flung open his door as well, causing Cruddy to bang into it with a clang. Both crows lay stunned on the floor.

But the minute they saw Sammy, Rodney and Mortimer step out from behind their doors, Crummy and Cruddy revived, then screamed, staggered to their feet and then turned and ran down the tunnel as fast as they could in the opposite direction.

"That's a big mistake," said Mortimer. "The tunnel turns into a labyrinth deep in the depths."

"A what?" asked Rodney.

"A labyrinth," said Sammy. "It's a bunch of joined paths branching off in many directions — pretty easy to get lost in it."

"The rabbits built it that way, to keep predators from tracking them," said Mortimer. "But that was a long time ago. Now I hear some skunk has made his home at the exit to the labyrinth. Those two crows won't want to meet up with him, I'm sure."

"I'll bet that's Squirty Skunk!" said Rodney.

"He'll give them a skunky squirt or two, and those two crows will get what they deserve," laughed Sammy. "Now let's find Judy."

"Over here!" Judy cried out, hearing the sound of familiar voices.

Sammy and Rodney hurried over to a nearby door and opened it. A very happy Judy Crow looked up at them from the bottom of a pit.

"Sammy and Rodney! Oh, it's so good to see familiar faces!" exclaimed Judy.

"Don't worry, Judith. We're going to get you out of there," said Sammy.

"Oh, thank you, my friend…and…please call me Judy. I don't know why I wanted everyone to call me Judith. I've been such a cantankerous crow, haven't I?"

"No one's perfect, Judy," said Rodney. "Sammy made that clear to me. Can you fly out of there?

"No, I can't. When the crow-nappers hauled me over here they injured my wing."

"So sorry to hear that," said Mortimer, joining Sammy and Rodney at the doorway.

"I think we'll need your help again," said Sammy. "Judy, this is Mortimer Mole. He's the night security patrol. Rodney will hang onto Mortimer's feet and lower himself down. Then I'll climb down and hang on to Rodney's tail. We'll look a bit like a totem pole in Stanley Park, but you should be able to hop over us to the top."

Mortimer held on to the door frame, then sat on the pit edge and lowered his legs again. This time, Rodney climbed down. Then Sammy scrambled down both of them and gripped Rodney's tail.

"Here I come," said Judy Crow, as she hopped up and grabbed Sammy's tail. Then she continued up Sammy's back, over Rodney and reached the top. "I've made it!" she yelled back down.

So Sammy and Rodney hauled themselves up, and Judy rushed to give them each a big hug.

"You're amazing friends, you two," said Judy as she shed a tear. "I've been a cranky old crow to you before, but I've changed. Thank you, Sammy and Rodney...and you too, Mortimer Mole."

"All in a night's duty, ma'am," replied Mortimer. "Let me escort all of you back to the inn. You must be exhausted."

After Sammy and Rodney said good-night and went to their room, Mortimer took Judy to the front desk and quickly arranged a small room for her. She thanked him once again, and retired for the night. As Mortimer moseyed down the hallway to continue his duties he muttered to himself, "And I took this job because of the peace and quiet….Who knew, who knew…."

9

On the Way Back

Sammy, Rodney and Judy met at the front desk early in the morning to check out of the inn. They thanked Fernando Fox for his kindness and hospitality.

"Oh, you're more than welcome," said Fernando, "and on behalf of the Animal Inn, may I say how sorry I am about the difficult situation you've endured, Ms. Crow."

"That's very kind," replied Judy. "And I must say that Mortimer Mole was so helpful to us."

Many thanks and good-byes were exchanged, and they made their way out of the inn.

"Well, I suppose we should go back the way we came," said Sammy.

"Why don't we take a different route," Rodney suggested. "Instead of walking by the seawall path, why don't we meander through this maze of tall buildings on our way back to the park?"

"Oh, I don't know," replied Sammy. "There might be a lot of people and pets in that area. I don't think we should push our luck."

"I don't think we have anything to worry about," said Judy. "I've flown over this street many times and it always looked quite safe. Besides, it's too early for people and pets to be out and about."

"Surely a short jaunt through the area won't do us any harm," added Rodney. "I think Lost Lagoon is just on the other side of those apartment buildings where all the people and pets live. We'll be in the park much faster than by taking the seawall route."

"Well okay, if you two insist," replied Sammy. "But I don't have a good feeling about this."

So they started on their way and walked past several lofty buildings, down an attractive tree-lined street. Some buildings had grassy patches in front of them and others had flower gardens.

"There, look how lovely this is," Rodney said happily. "Enjoy yourself. Smell the grass and the flowers."

And the smell was really quite agreeable, which put the three animal friends in a very good mood. They could see towering trees and lush vegetation at the end of the long street and realized that was the edge of Stanley

Park. In a very short while they would be safe in the woodland refuge, surrounded by the gigantic trees of home.

There was, however, something else at the end of the street that looked unfamiliar. Sammy spotted it first, but didn't say anything to Rodney or Judy because he thought he was imagining things. Then the other two animals saw it.

"Is that some type of small deer up ahead?" asked Judy.

"I was going to ask you the same thing," replied Rodney.

Just then, the unusual looking animal started to move in their direction. As it came closer, Rodney felt a lump of fear in the pit of his stomach.

"That's no deer," he said nervously. "It's a…you know…a…a…Botherman Snitcher, or…or whatever they're called."

Sammy and Judy knew exactly what Rodney was trying to say. 'Botherman Snitcher' wasn't the right term for the breed of dog that was advancing, but the three animal friends were now so afraid they couldn't think of the correct name. The black and tan dog had pointy ears, a slim muscular body and fierce eyes that were focussed directly on the three of them. Within seconds, the Doberman Pinscher — which was the correct name — stood in front of them and blocked their path.

"Good morning, kind dog," said Sammy rather meekly, as he looked up at the ferocious creature. Rodney and Judy stood silently frozen behind Sammy.

"Well, well, well," said the dog with a menacing grin. "Just what do we have here? Two little animals and a wounded bird, by my reckoning. What brings three defenceless park critters into my territory?"

"Oh, is this your territory?" said Rodney, trying to sound as pleasant and amiable as he could. "We must have made a wrong turn…so sorry. We'll just go back the way we came and enter the park another way."

"Just a moment," interrupted the large dog in a sinister voice. "I might consider letting you through my street…or two of you anyway." He started to laugh. It was a deep and powerful laugh that erupted from the dog, and it made the little animals shiver.

As the three friends gave each other a quick look, the dog snarled and stepped forward. That's when they knew they were trapped, and that there was no point in running because this dog was clearly built for speed.

"Get behind that tree over there!" shouted Sammy, pointing it out to his friends. Then he ran up a nearby trunk as fast as he could.

Startled by the speed of the squirrel, the Doberman momentarily froze, then bounded toward the trunk.

"Come down from there you little shrimp or I'll eat your friends for lunch!"

As Rodney and Judy quivered behind a neighbouring tree, a crab apple suddenly fell directly in front of the dog. He looked up at Sammy in surprise. Just then, a second crab apple fell, landing directly on the canine's head.

"Bull's eye!" Sammy yelled. Then another apple hit the dog on the rump, and suddenly it was raining apples on the dog, hitting him all over.

"Ouch!" yelled the dog. "Stop it! Ouch!"

"Run, you two, run!" shouted Sammy as the dog backed away from the tree. Without hesitation, Rodney and Judy ran down the street as fast as they could, not even once turning their heads to see if the dog was following them. They ran and ran and ran, half-expecting to be picked up by the scruff of the neck and turned into Botherman Snitcher stew. But nothing of the sort happened because while they ran, Sammy scrambled over the tree branches and pitched crab apples at the Doberman.

Exhausted and panting, Rodney and Judy finally stopped running when they reached the entrance to the park. They looked back and were relieved to see Sammy scampering down the sidewalk to meet them and the dog running in the opposite direction.

"Well done!" said Judy.

"Well, that was a bit of luck!" added Rodney.

"No thanks to you, Rodney Raccoon. I told you I didn't want to take this route," said Sammy angrily. "Renee Rabbit warned us about unleashed pets before we left the park. We could have been devoured right then and there."

"But we weren't, were we?" replied Rodney. "Sometimes you have to take a chance and let serendipity happen."

Rodney stopped walking and broke into laughter. "I remembered it! I remembered it!" he said excitedly. "And now I know what it means. I really do!"

"Remembered what?" said a very irritated Sammy Squirrel.

"Remembered the word 'serendipity.' It's that word you used when we arrived at the Sylvia Hotel," said Rodney, still laughing. "I guess I'm a smarter raccoon than I thought. When I saw that dog, I thought we were in the wrong place at the wrong time, but we were standing beneath the crab apple tree, which, under the circumstances, meant we were in the right place at the right time because you ran up there and started chucking all those apples at him. That's serendipity. Don't you see?"

Sammy sighed. "I see only one thing," he said, "and it's ahead of us. It's called Stanley Park. You do remember that, don't you?

"Yes, of course," Rodney replied.

"Well then, do you think we can go home…without any more meandering?"

"Let's go," Rodney replied, "before I get too hungry to walk."

10

Food and Friends

Turning away from the street, they entered Stanley Park and headed for the very first animal trail they saw. Once they were on the familiar path, the three little animals slowed their walking pace and breathed in the fresh, moist air. They looked up and around them with awe and gratitude at the enormous trees. They were in their home park — safe and protected by the abundant nature all around them.

Rodney was hungry as usual, so he suggested they take the trail that would lead them to Lost Lagoon. Rows and rows of huckleberry and blackberry bushes could be found there, and a quick stop would temporarily satisfy his hunger. Sammy and Judy didn't have much of an appetite after the encounter with the Botherman Snitcher, but Rodney insisted.

On the way down the hill to the lagoon, Sammy

noticed a peculiar thing. There was a maple tree ahead of them that appeared to be smiling through its leaves. Knowing full well that trees are not the smiling type due to the fact that they are vegetation, this seemed quite strange.

"Do you see that maple tree up ahead along the trail, Rodney?" Sammy asked.

"What…you mean the one over there that's smiling at us?" Then, realizing what he'd just said, Rodney shouted, "Sammy, Judy, look! There's a tree up ahead and it's smiling. How can that be?"

"So you see it, too," said Judy. "Well, at least I'm not the only one. I often see trees that appear to be smiling at me when I'm flying through the park. Do you think that tree over there is happy to see us?"

"Maybe it is, or maybe it's just having a good day," replied Rodney, "and maybe we've never noticed that trees smile when they're in a good mood."

"I'm inclined to think it's an optical illusion," said Sammy. "It's probably just the way the light is coming through the branches. It's kind of like how the moon at night appears to have a smiling face."

"You mean to tell me that the moon doesn't really smile at us?" asked Rodney, now quite dismayed. "All these years, I was sure that was a friendly old moon up there. Now you're saying it's a tropical confusion…or whatever you called it."

"An optical illusion," said Sammy. "That's when your eyes play a trick on you and something appears to be very different from what it actually is."

"Oh, right," said Rodney. "That happens to me a lot. I often think I see berries on bushes up ahead when I'm out walking, but by the time I get there, I realize I've been having some kind of tropical confusion…I mean, optical illusion."

"Yes, it's something like that," said Sammy. "Well, let's be on our way, shall we?"

They moved along the trail until they came to the crest of a small hill. They walked down the hill and entered the wide path that wound its way around Lost Lagoon. Now they could see the ducks, swans and other water-fowl out on parade. When the lagoon birds spotted Sammy and Rodney escorting Judy Crow into the park, they hopped out of the water and rushed over. The three voyagers were surrounded by waterfowl of all shapes and sizes.

"Oh, Judy…I mean…Judith. You're all right!" said Dolores Duck.

"Yes, I'm fine — thanks to Rodney and Sammy. And call me Judy, won't you?" Judy then explained to the excited birds what had happened and how the two brave little park animals had saved her.

"Hurray for Sammy Squirrel and Rodney Raccoon!" shouted Penelope Pigeon, who happened to be tap-dancing in the area and had overheard the whole story. "I never thought Rodney was capable of anything like this, but I have to admit I was wrong about him."

Penelope started to sing and was quickly joined by all the birds in attendance:

For these are jolly good animals
For these are jolly good animals
For these are jolly good animals
Which no critter can deny!

Which no critter can deny
Which no critter can deny
For these are jolly good animals
Which no critter can deny!

All the animals laughed and cheered when the song finished.

"It's so good to see our fellow park animals," said Sammy. "You have no idea how good it is."

The geese, ducks, swans and other lagoon residents

were curious. They had never been out of the park before and swamped Sammy, Rodney and Judy with questions.

"How dangerous was it?" quacked a duck.

"Did you encounter many people and pets?" sang a swan.

"What's going to happen to those nasty crows that did this to Judy?" honked a goose.

"I think I took care of that," said Squirty Skunk, who had heard the singing and had come running over. "I gave them a very skunky squirt when they dashed through my den at the labyrinth's end. They flew off in a very stinky state!"

"That's great news. I would have hopped over to help, if I'd only known," croaked a frog.

"I have several little city friends in that area," squeaked a mouse. "They could have helped too!"

The questions and comments were fired all at once, leaving little room for answers or replies.

"Wait a minute, wait a minute!" said Rodney. "Let's just say that it was an adventure, a real adventure for all three of us. It was dangerous at times, yes, but we met a couple of animals at the inn who were very kind and helpful. We also met a rather nasty dog on the way home."

"Well, the three of you must be tired after your city adventure," said Dolores. "You should go back to your

homes now and get some rest. We can pepper you with questions another time."

Nodding in agreement, the three friends said good-bye and left Lost Lagoon. They walked down the trail that took them away from the outskirts and into the heart of Stanley Park. They were back where they belonged, and with each step they felt calmer and happier. Sammy and Rodney escorted Judy back to her tree where the sign proclaiming *Judith Raven's Residence* hung proudly from a high branch.

"I'm going to change that sign," said Judy. "I'm going to change it to *Judy Crow — Proud Friend of Sammy Squirrel and Rodney Raccoon*. What do you think of that?"

"We would be honoured, Judy," said Sammy. "Thank you."

"Yes, we would indeed," added Rodney. "Now, go have some rest, my dear. Sammy and I are quite hungry and must gather up some things to eat."

"Food, food, food," said Sammy with a chuckle. "It's all he really thinks about."

"He does think about food frequently," remarked Judy. "But he clearly thinks about his friends a lot as well. Walk home safely, you two."

Sammy and Rodney bid adieu to Judy and went on their way. Along the trail, the two animal friends stopped to pick the wild huckleberries and blackberries.

"I'll just munch on a few berries while we're here," said Rodney, "to check the quality."

Having gathered enough for a hearty meal, they continued their trek toward Rodney's lair. Their plan was to have tree leaf tea and berries and rest their weary feet for awhile, after which Sammy would leave for his tree house deep in the park forest.

They arrived at Rodney's lair, made their way into the kitchen, then plunked their pile of berries on the table. Sammy made a pot of tree leaf tea, while Rodney washed the berries they had gathered. Tea made and berries cleaned, they sat in two armchairs in front of the hearth, embraced by the glow of the warm fire.

"That was quite an adventure, wasn't it?" sighed Rodney, as he sipped his tea.

"It certainly was," replied Sammy. "I'm so glad we were able to help Judy. What would have happened if we hadn't gone to look for her?"

"Friends are important," said Rodney, now a bit drowsy. "We never really know what's going to happen in life…so we have to help each other when times are difficult."

"So true," agreed Sammy. "Sometimes you have to take a chance — just spring into action and do the right thing, don't you agree, Rodney? Rodney…? Don't you think so?"

But there was no reply from Rodney Raccoon. Exhausted from the journey, he had fallen asleep in his chair in front of the cozy fire. Sammy began to feel sleepy too, and his eyes started to close.

"Yes…help your friends," Sammy said as he drifted off. "It's important…And do the right thing…always… always…zzzz…zzzz."

And he fell into a deep, wonderful sleep.

D uane Lawrence lives in Vancouver, B.C. where he teaches high school French and enjoys regular walks in beautiful Stanley park. It was during one leisurely stroll in the park that he decided to write about the animals that live there. This is Duane's second story about Sammy and Rodney and their adventures. A third story is in the works. Duane taught English in central Japan for 9 years and was a high school French teacher in London, England for one year. In addition to English, Duane speaks French and Japanese.